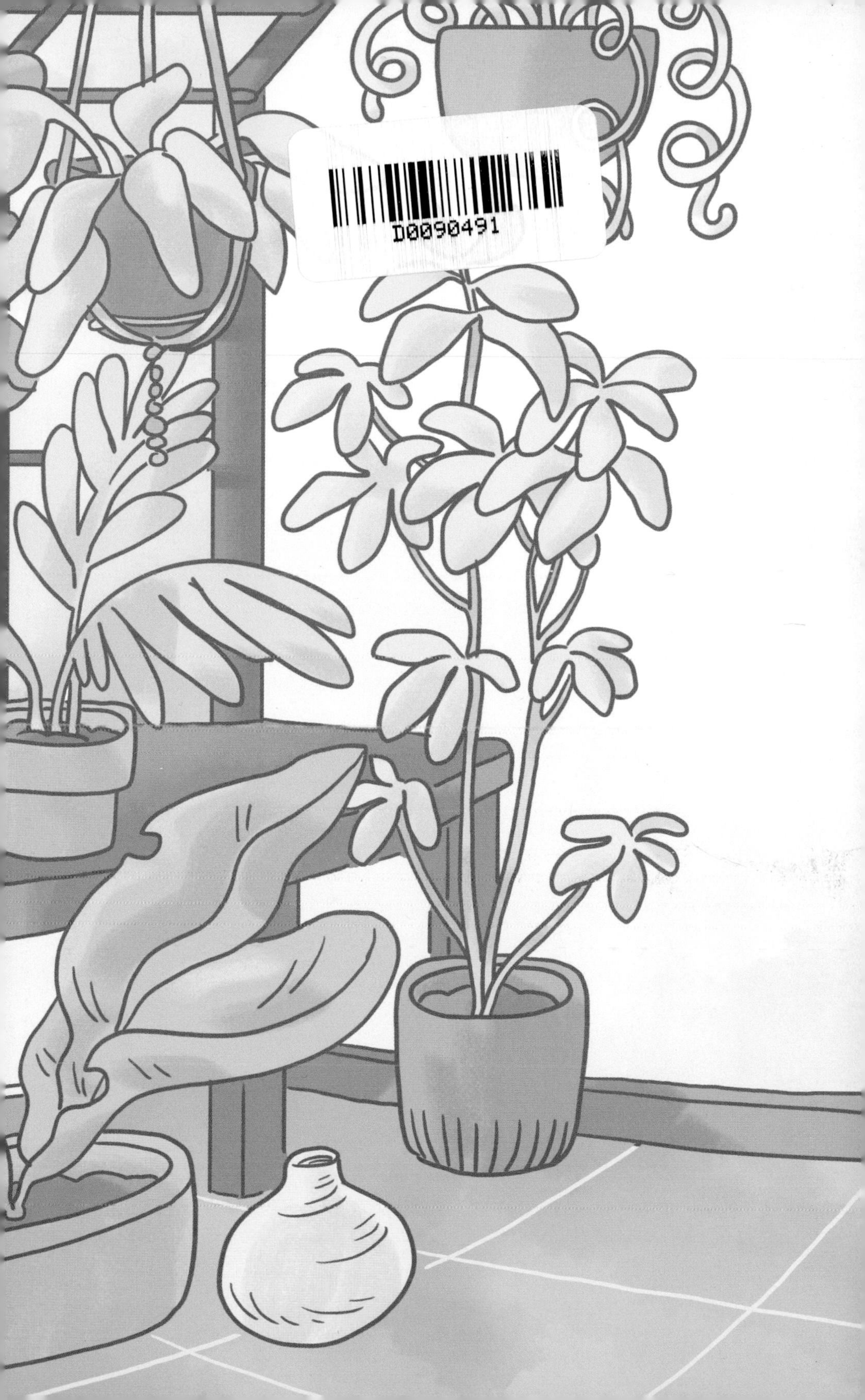

HOLIDAY HOUSE is registered in the U.S. Patent and Trademark Office.

Printed and bound in February 2021 at at Leo Paper, Heshan, China.

The art was created digitally.

www.holidayhouse.com

First Edition

1 3 5 7 9 10 8 6 4 2

Library of Congress Cataloging-in-Publication Data

Names: Knetzger, Laura, 1990– author.

Title: Five magic rooms / Laura Knetzger.

Description: New York : Holiday House, [2021] | Series: [I like to read
comics] | Audience: Ages 4–8. | Audience: Grades K–1. | Summary: When
Mia visits the home of her friend Pie, she is amazed by everything she
sees, feels, smells, and tastes, but Pie is sure that her home is just
as special.

Identifiers: LCCN 2020052651 | ISBN 9780823444977 (hardcover)

ISBN 9780823450442 (paperback)

Subjects: LCSH: Graphic novels. | CYAC: Graphic novels.

Dwellings—Fiction. | Friendship—Fiction.

Classification: LCC PZ7.7.K655 Fiv 2021 | DDC 741.5/973—dc23

LC record available at https://lccn.loc.gov/2020052651

ISBN: 978-0-8234-4497-7 (hardcover)

ISBN: 978-0-8234-5044-2 (paperback)

# MAGIC
# ROOMS

# LAURA KNETZGER

**HOLIDAY HOUSE · NEW YORK**

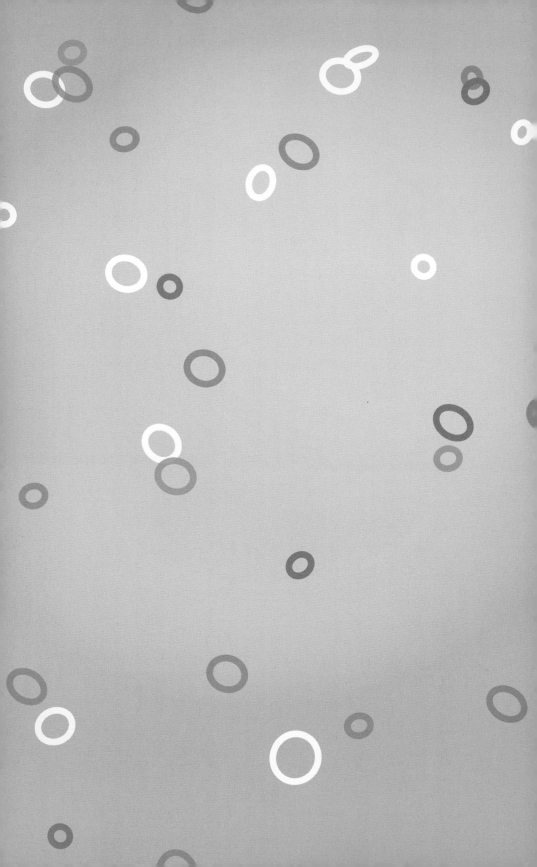

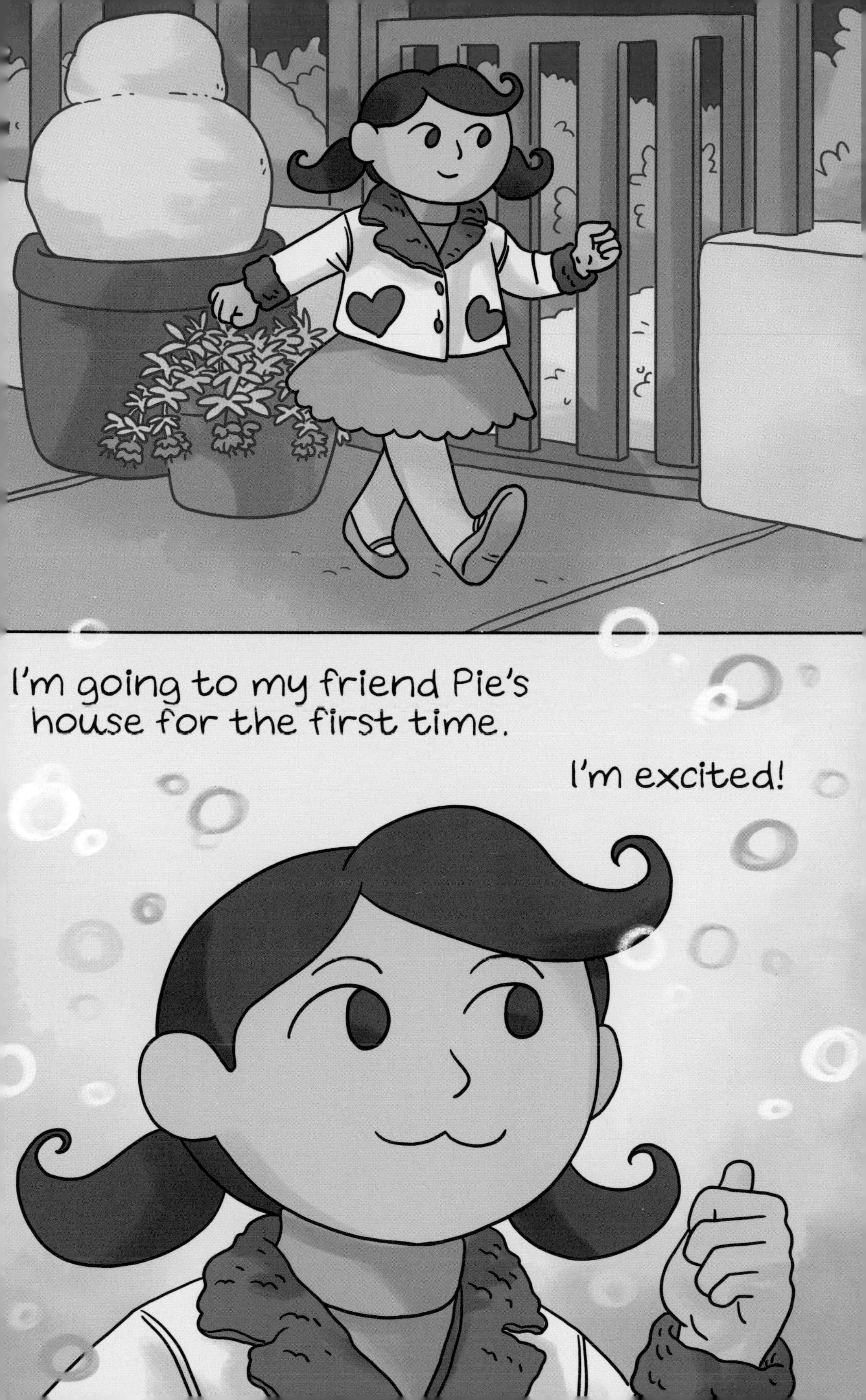
I'm going to my friend Pie's house for the first time.
I'm excited!

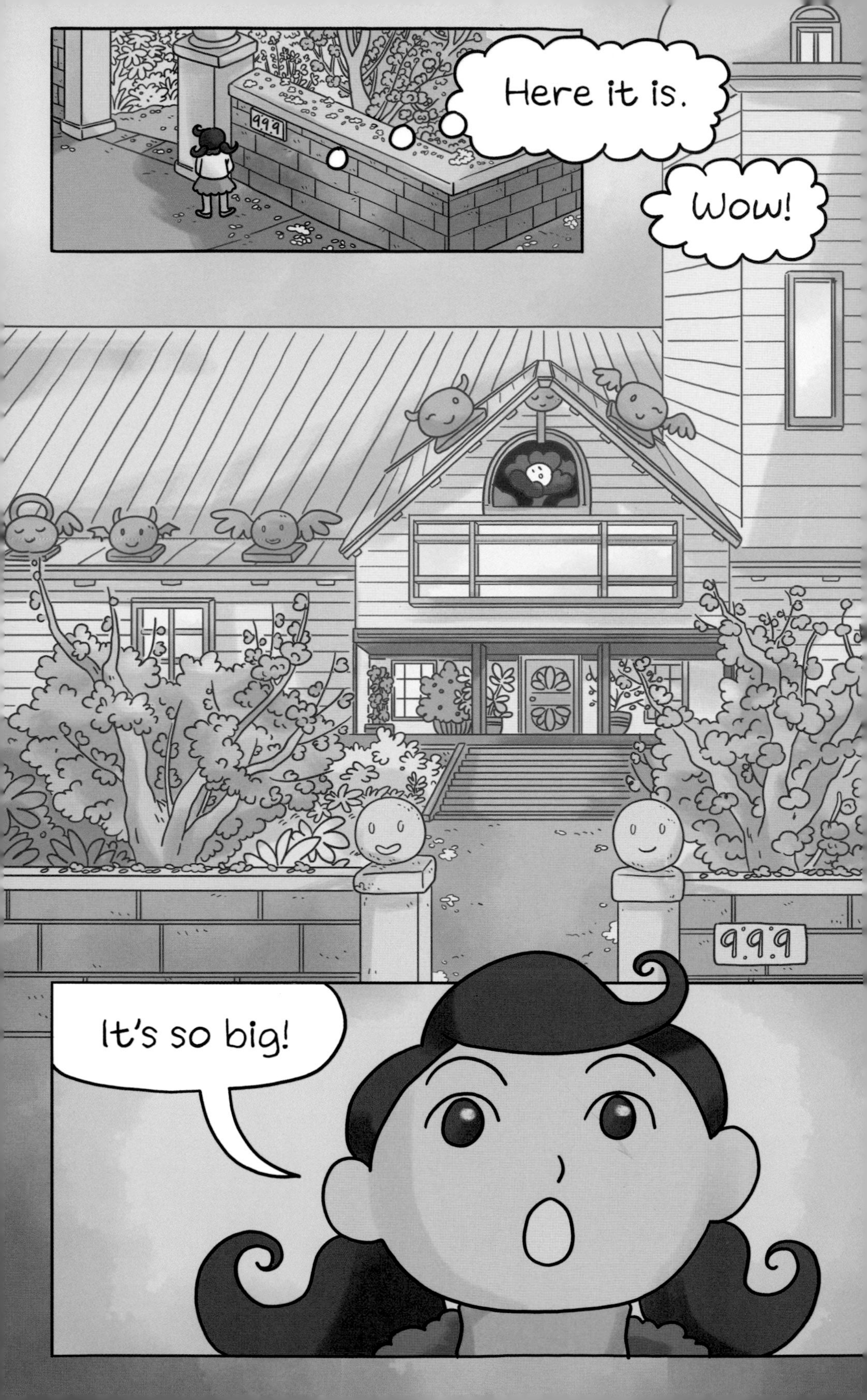

Here it is.
999
Wow!
999
It's so big!

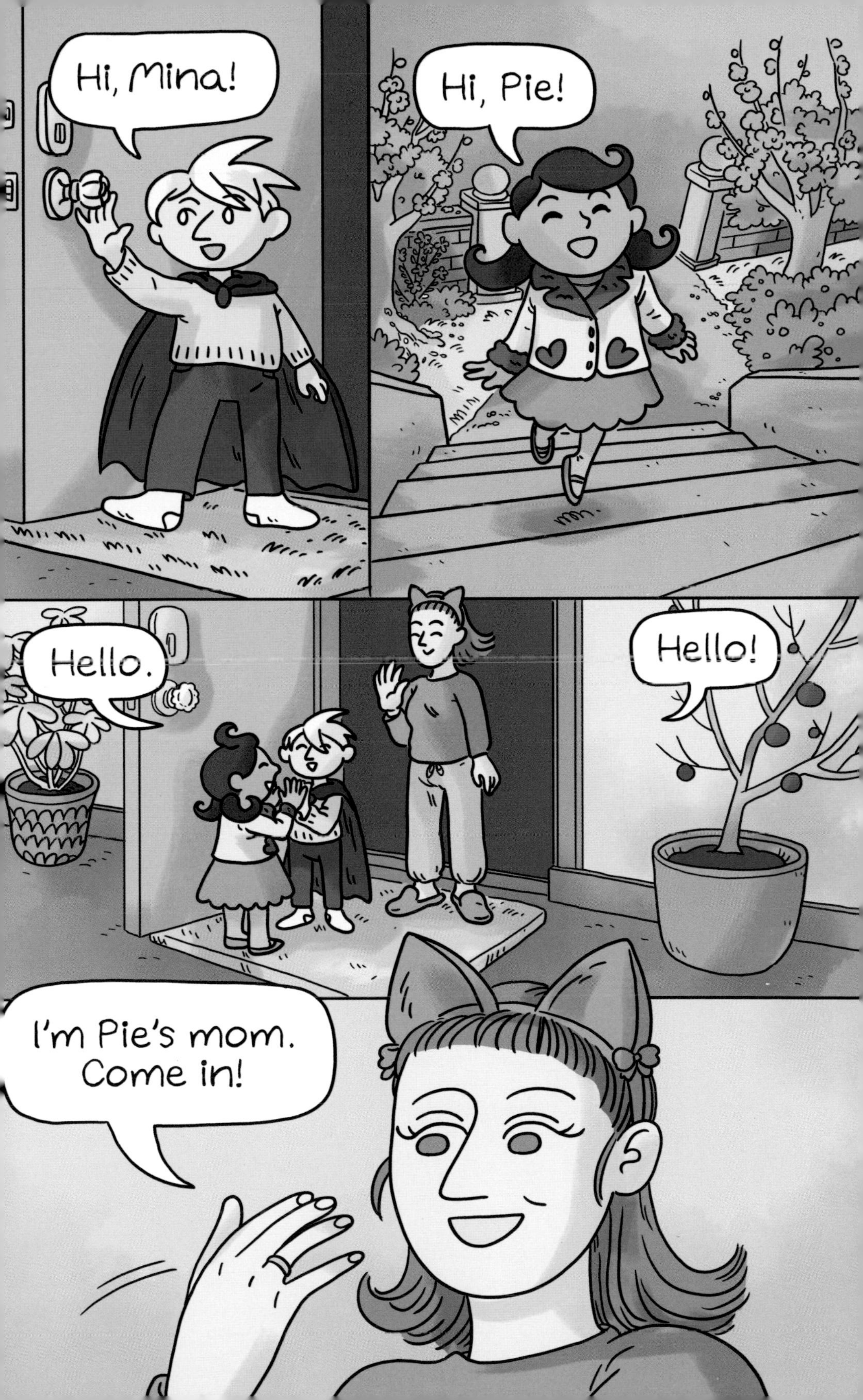
Hi, Mina!
Hi, Pie!
Hello.
Hello!
I'm Pie's mom.
Come in!

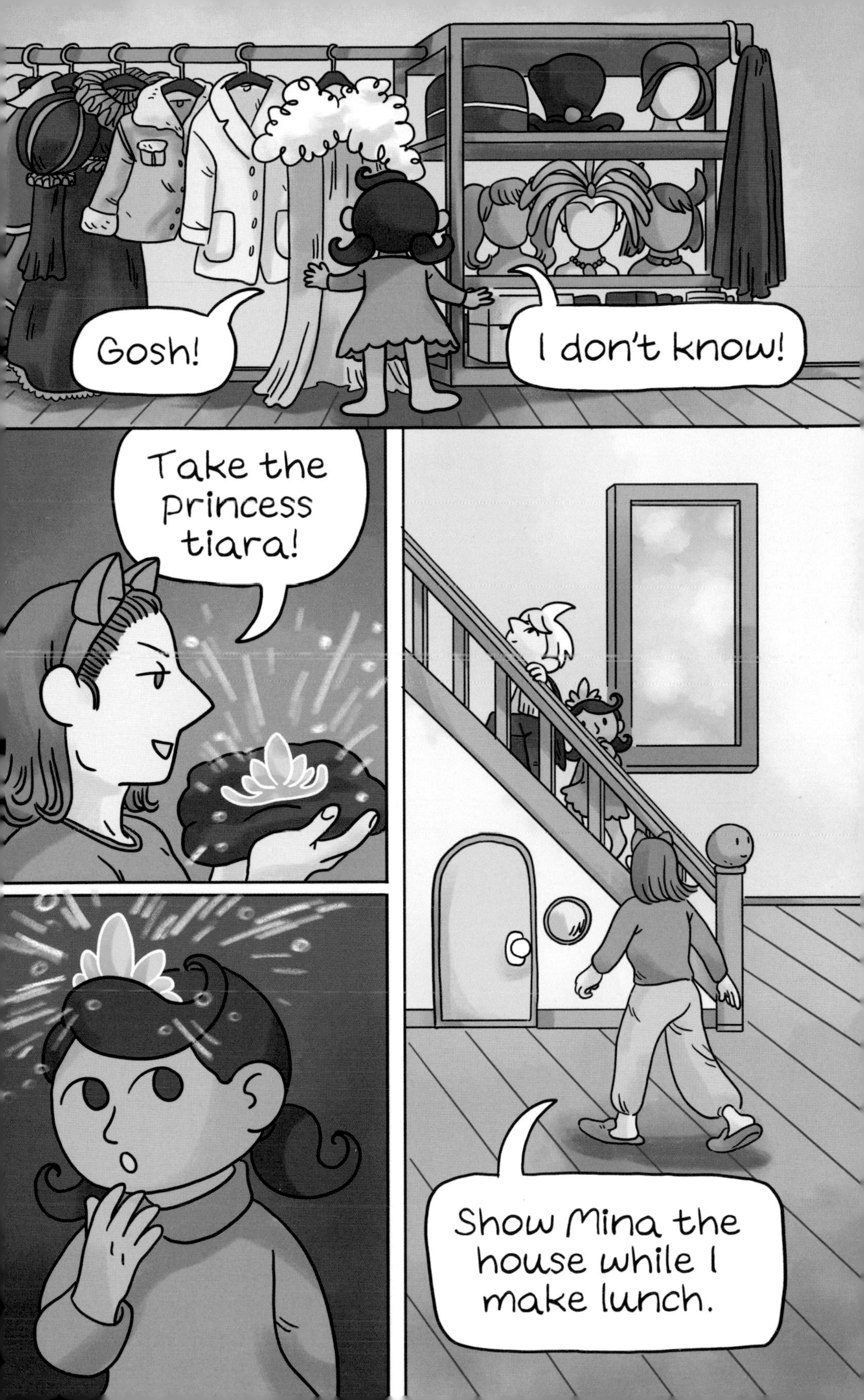
Gosh!
I don't know!
Take the princess tiara!
Show Mina the house while I make lunch.

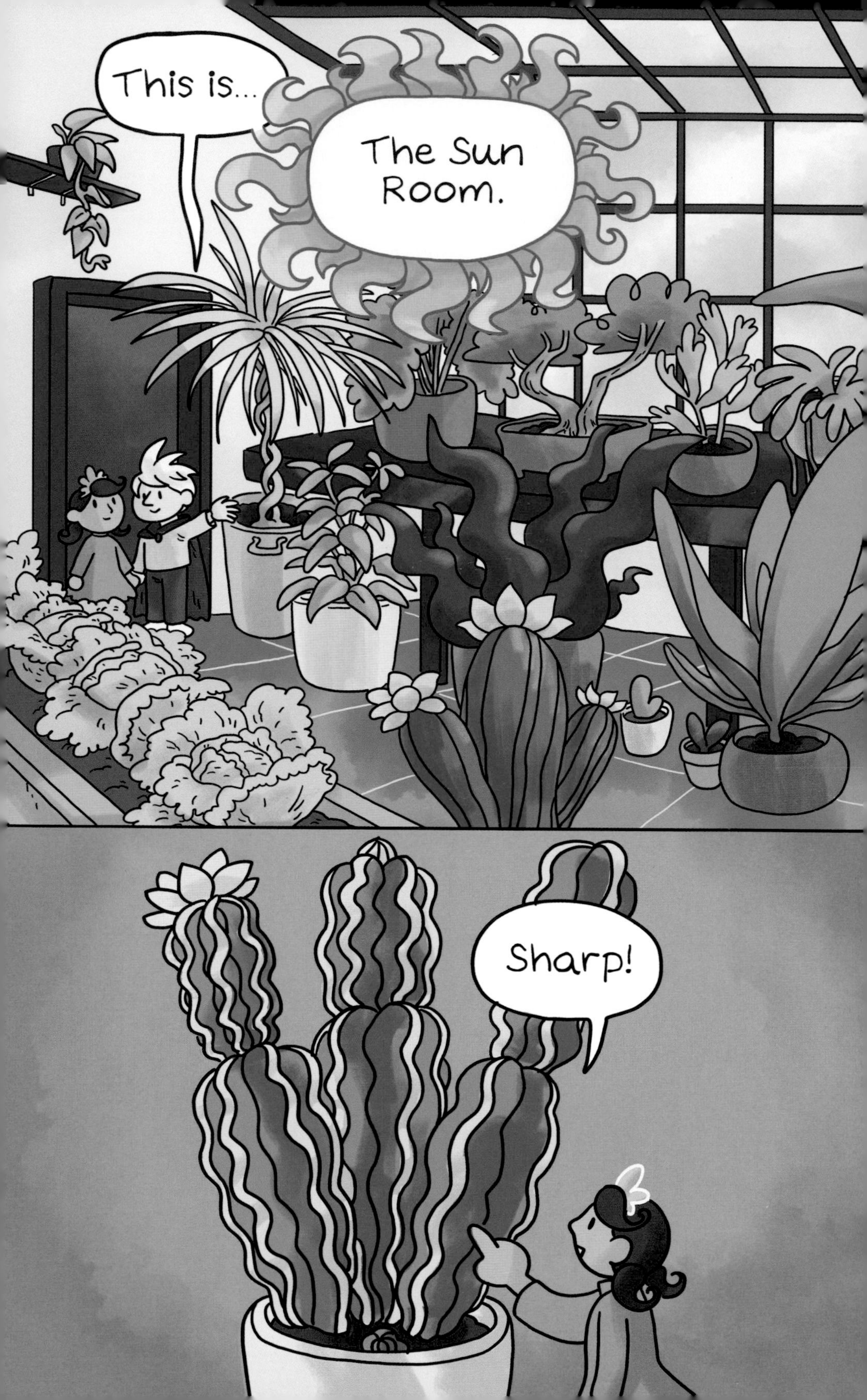
This is...
The Sun Room.
Sharp!

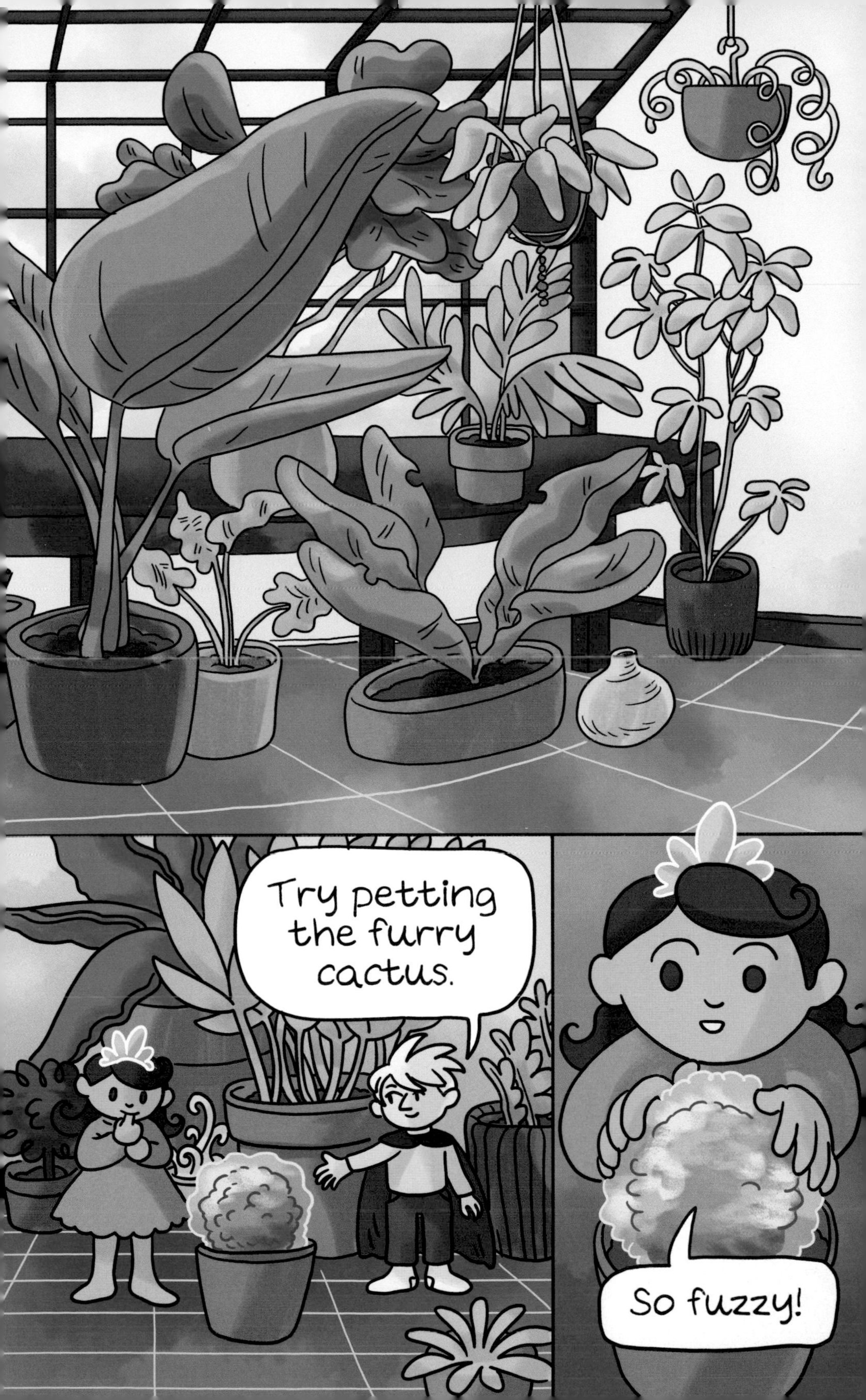
Try petting the furry cactus.
So fuzzy!

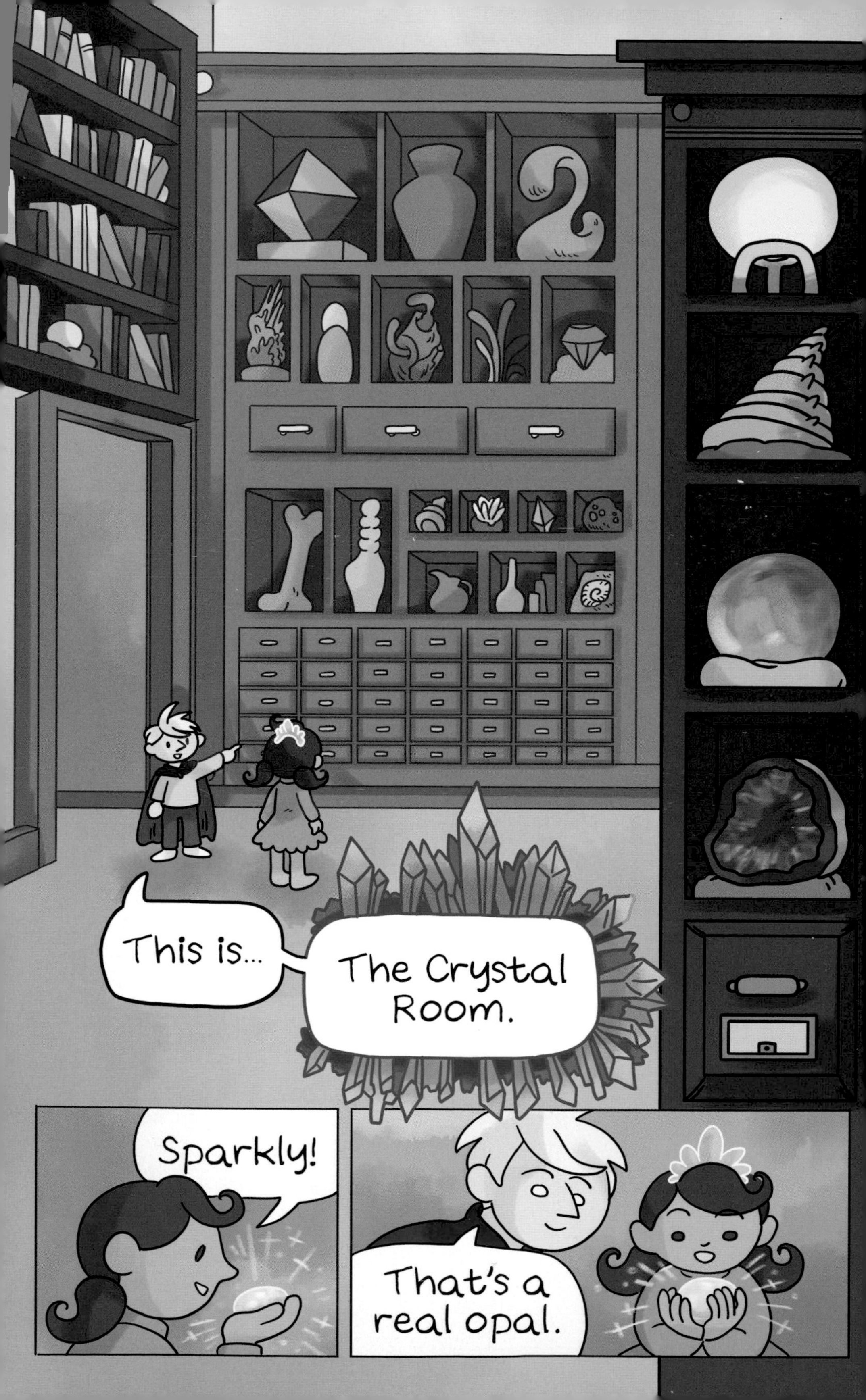
This is...
The Crystal Room.
Sparkly!
That's a real opal.

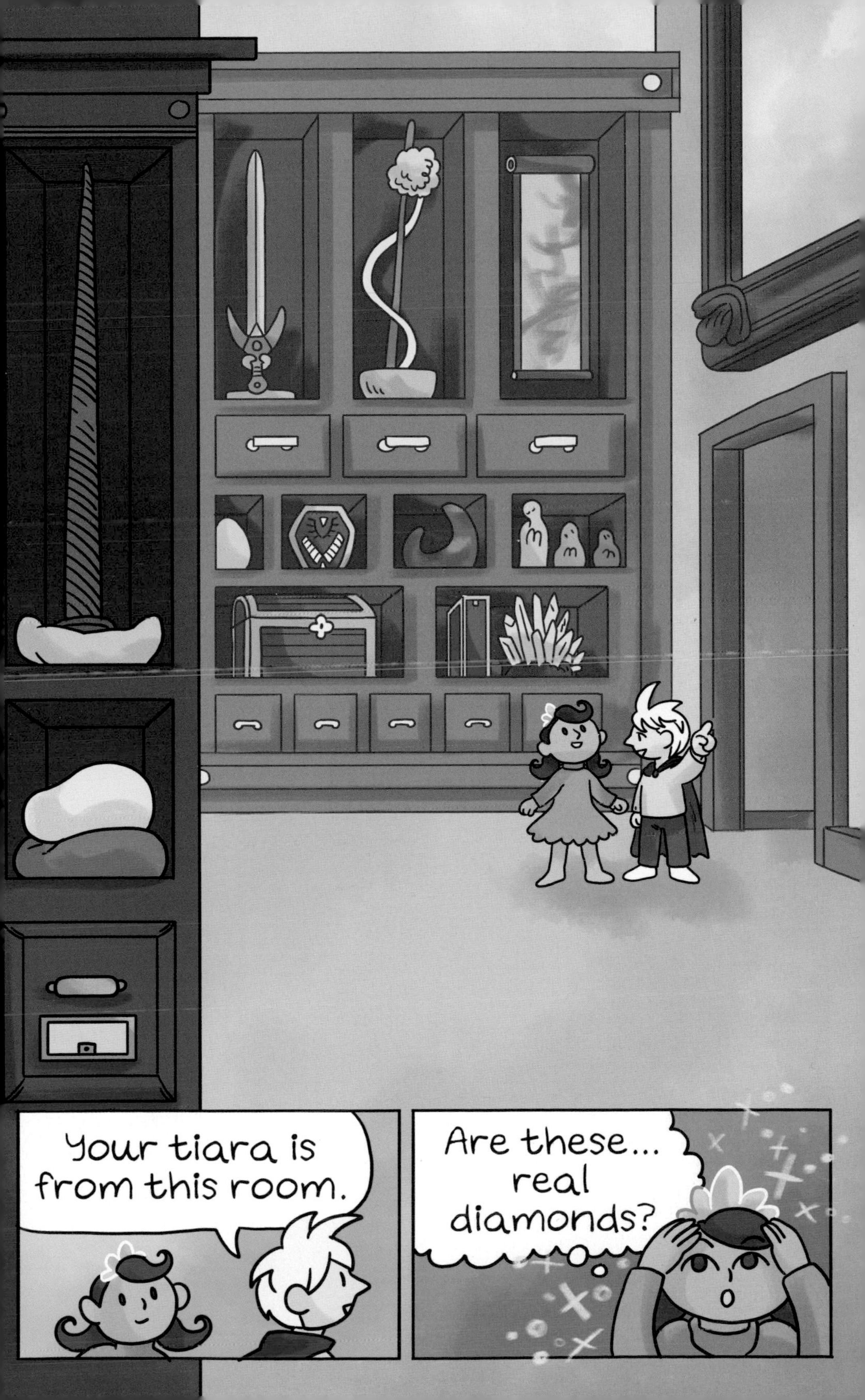
Your tiara is from this room.
Are these... real diamonds?

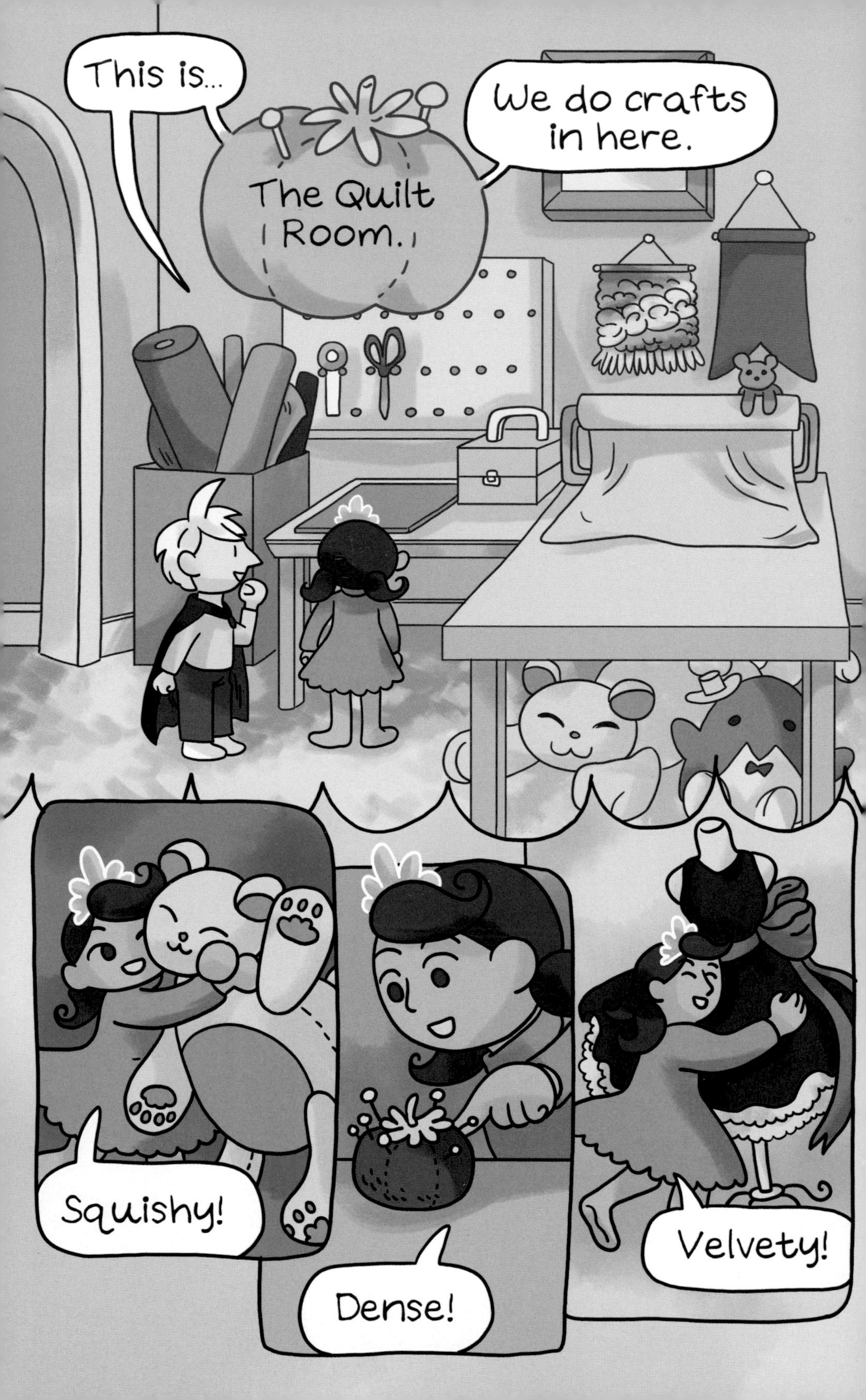
This is...
The Quilt Room.
We do crafts in here.
Squishy!
Dense!
Velvety!

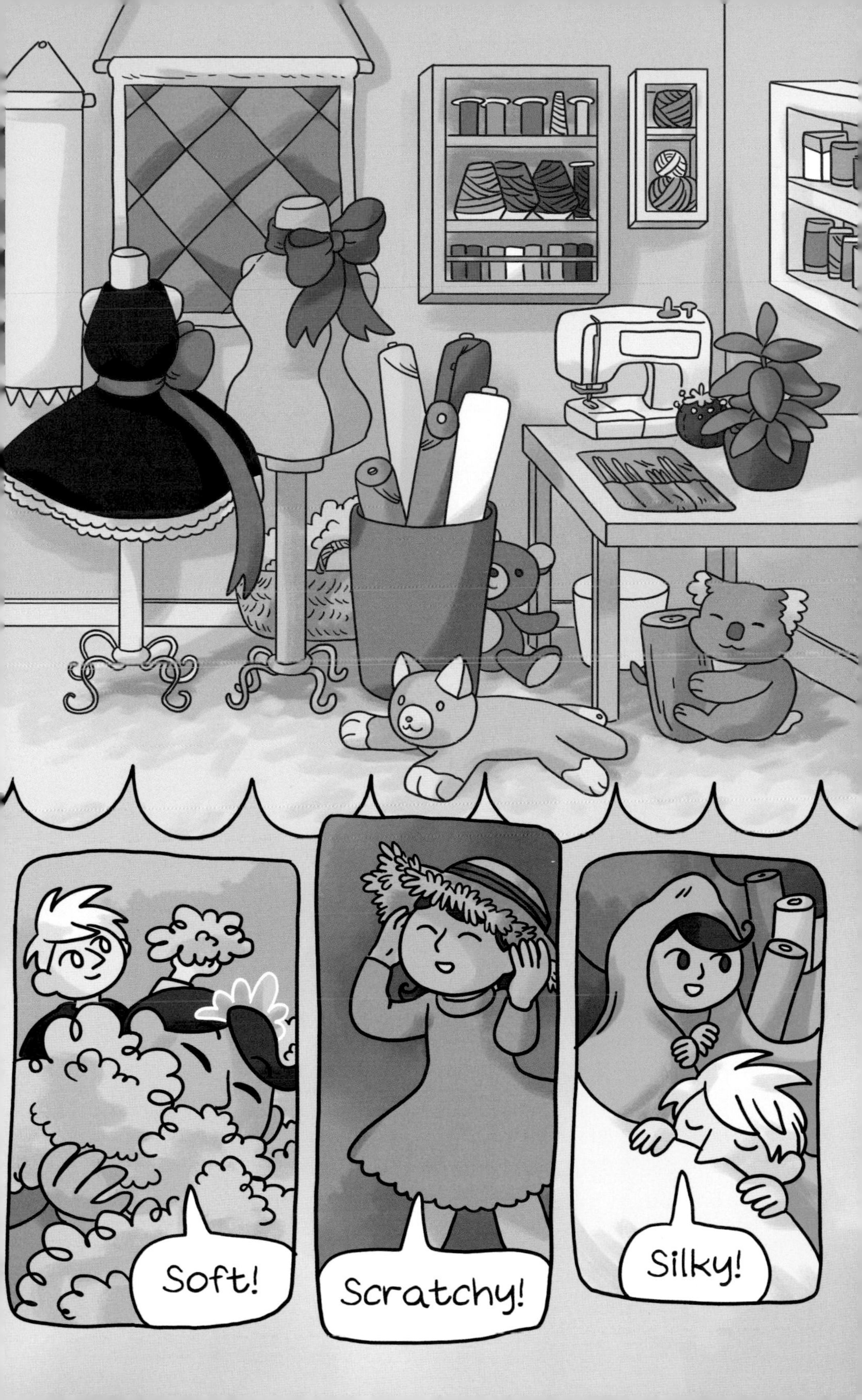
Soft!
Scratchy!
Silky!

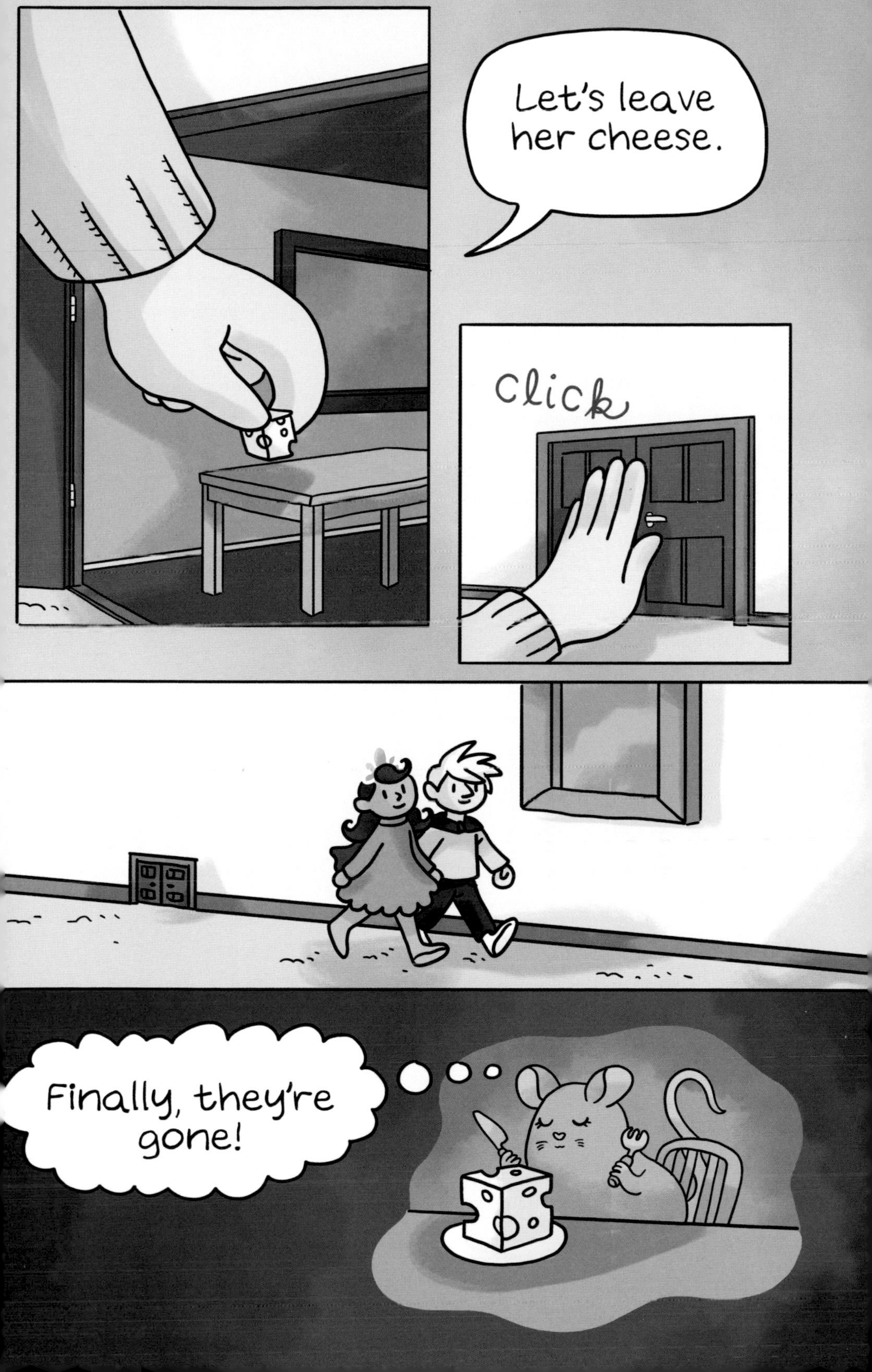
Let's leave her cheese.
Click
Finally, they're gone!

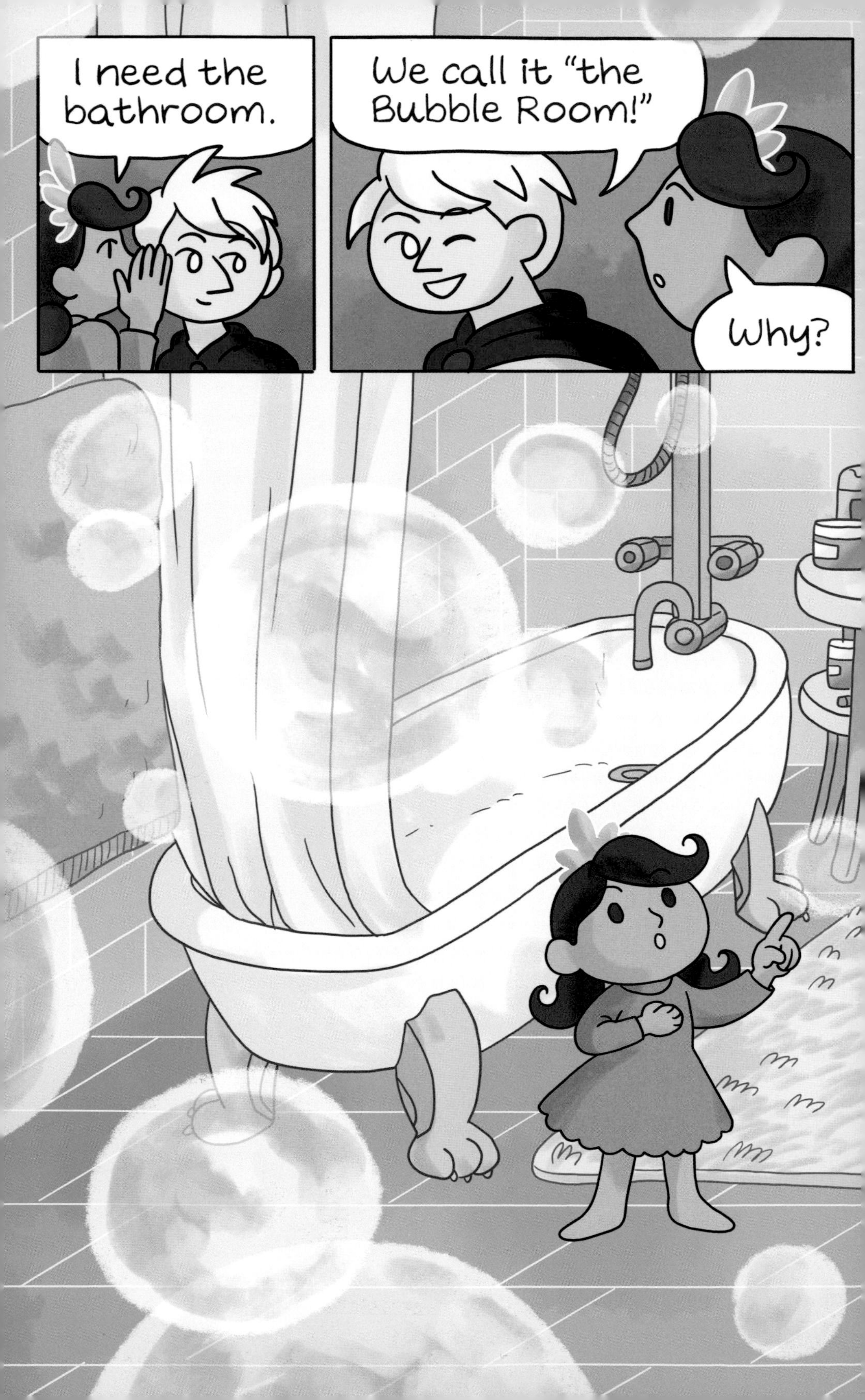
I need the bathroom.
We call it "the Bubble Room!"
Why?

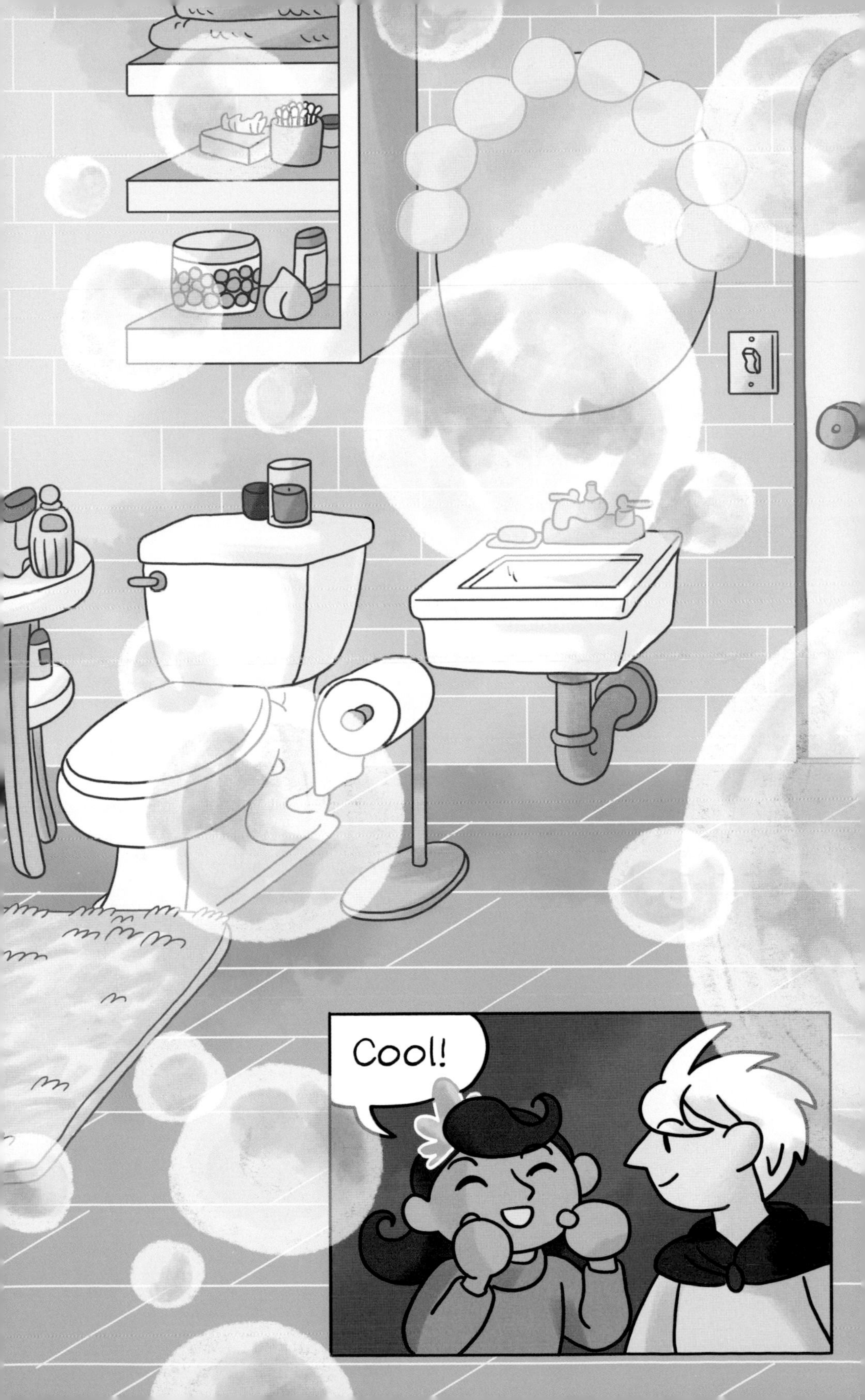
Cool!

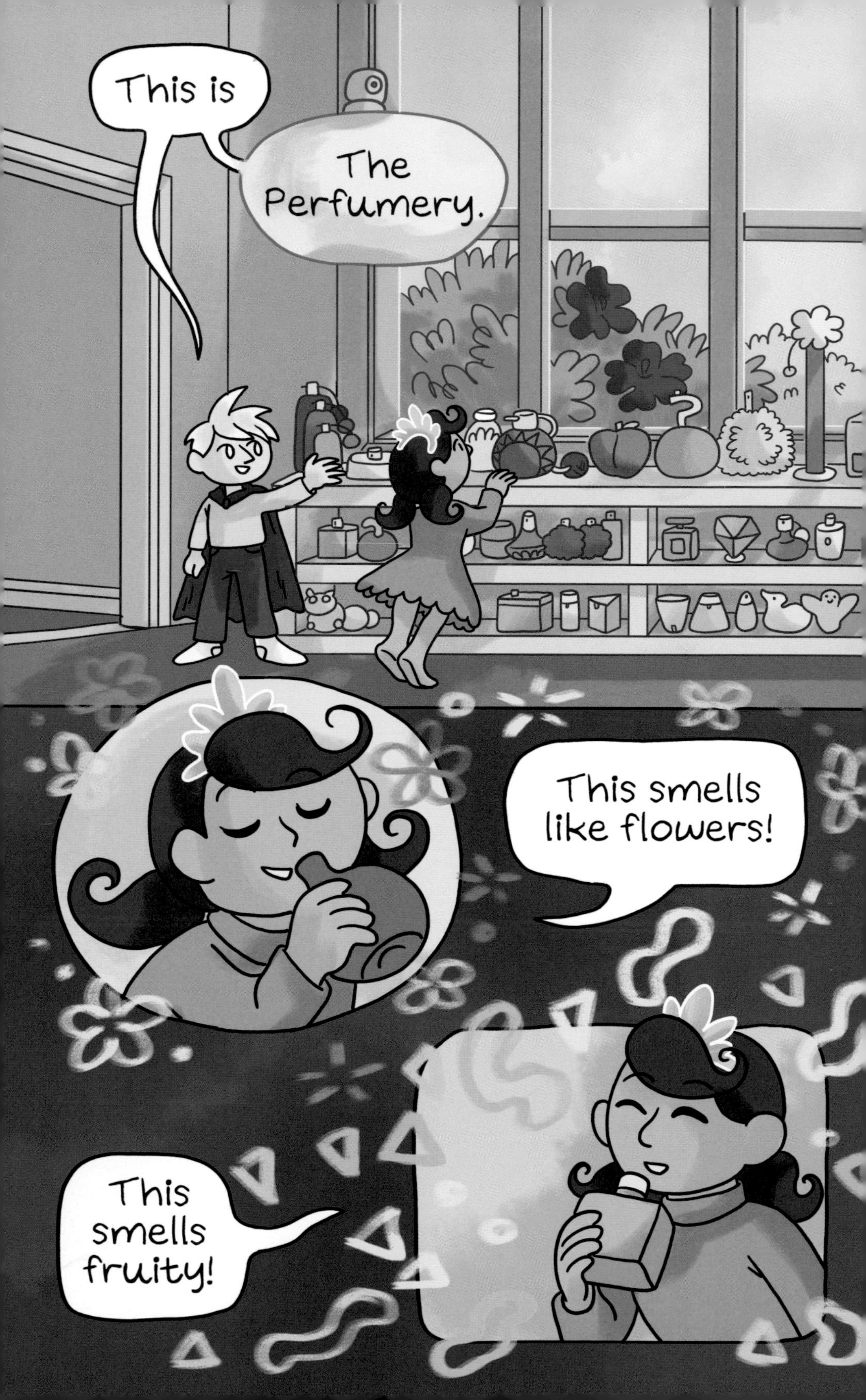
This is
The Perfumery.
This smells like flowers!
This smells fruity!

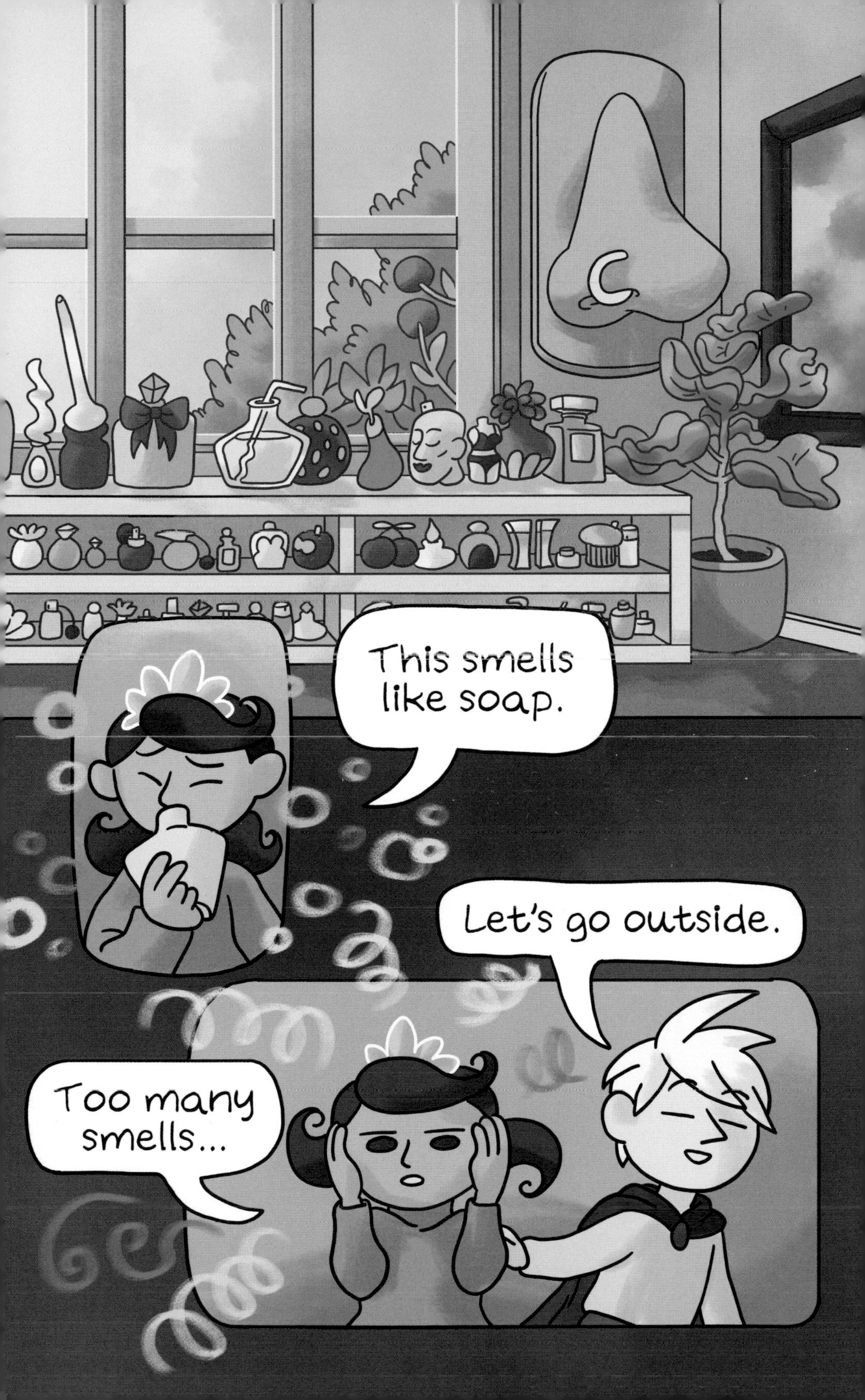
This smells like soap.
Let's go outside.
Too many smells...

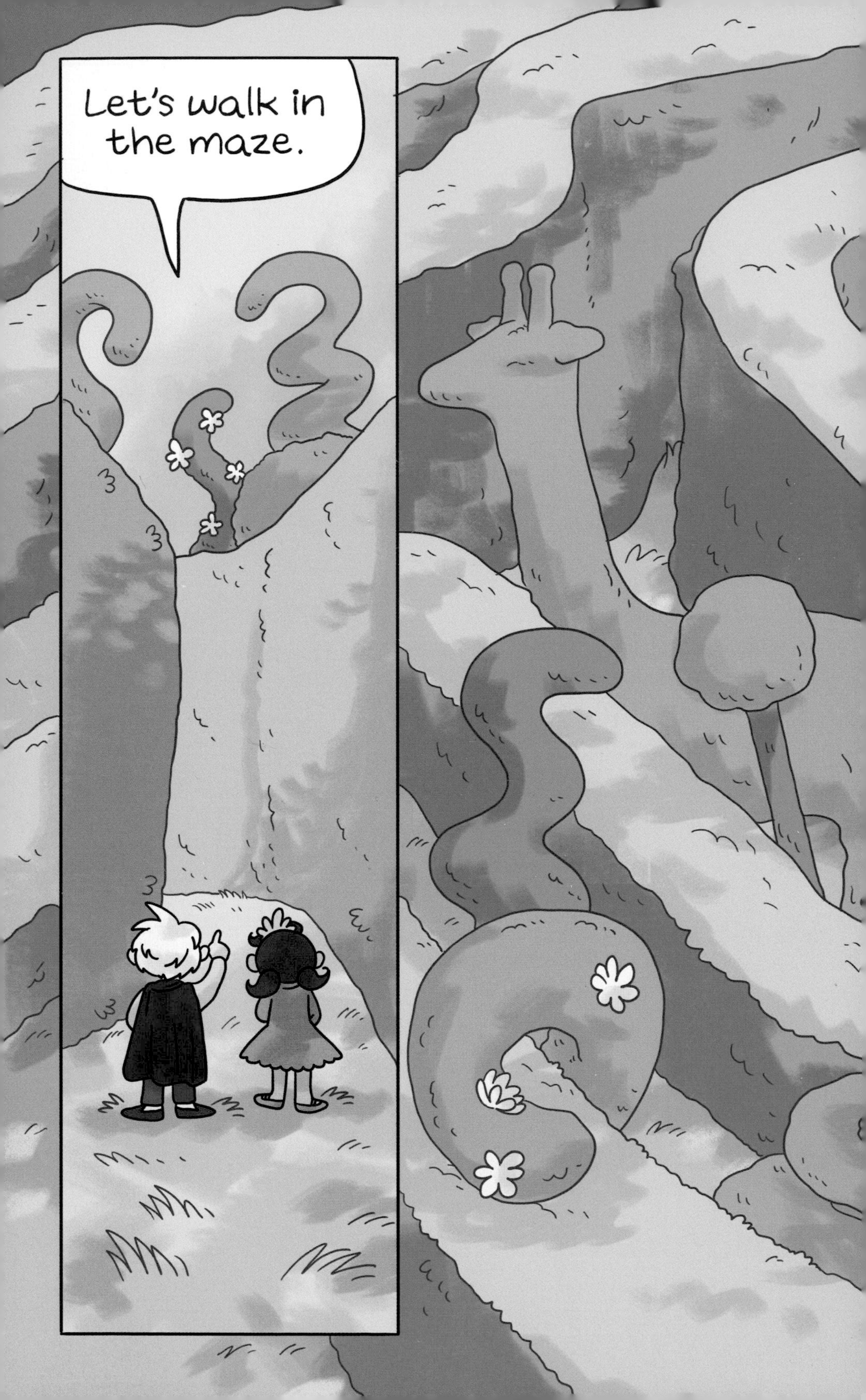
Let's walk in the maze.

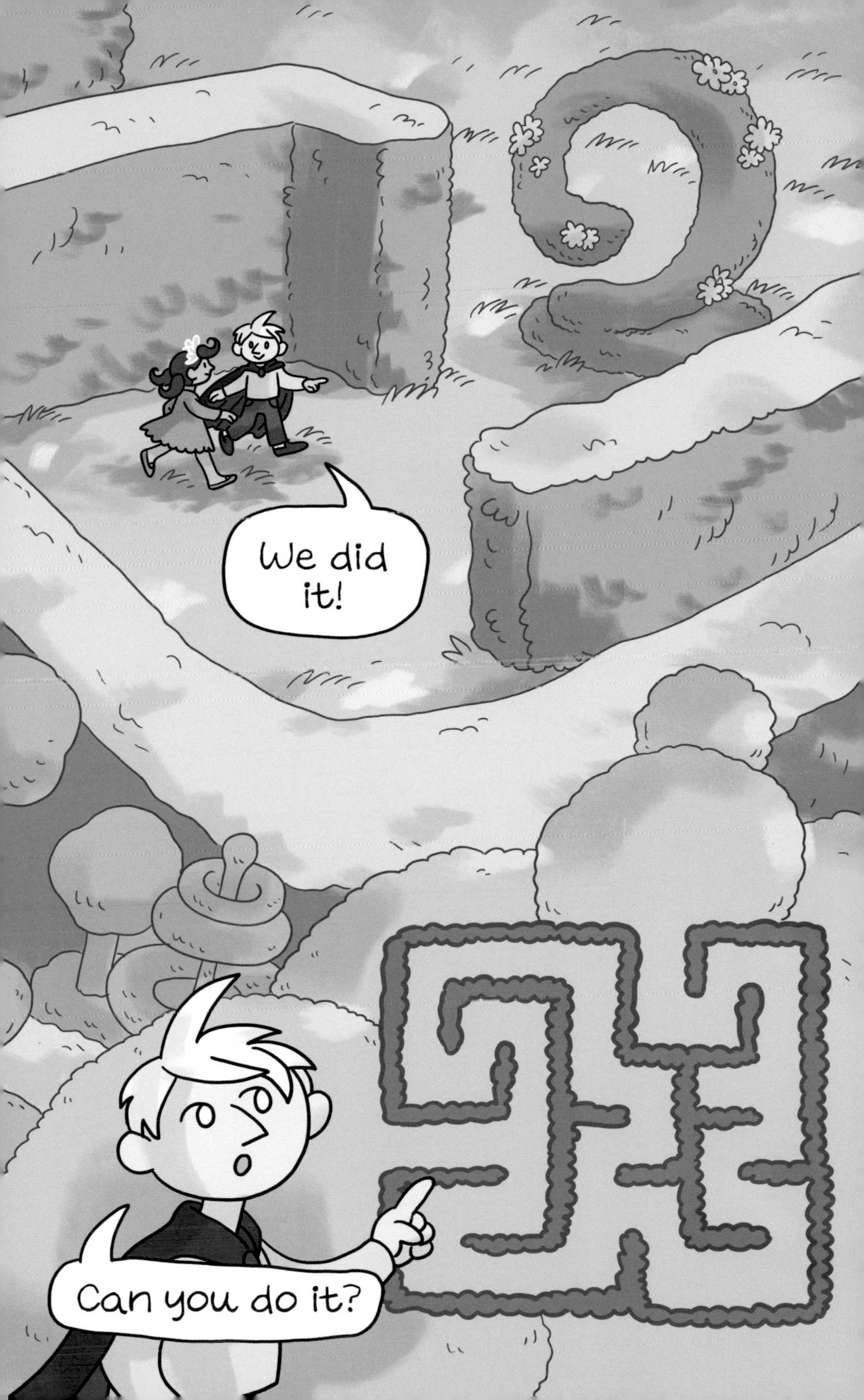
We did it!
Can you do it?

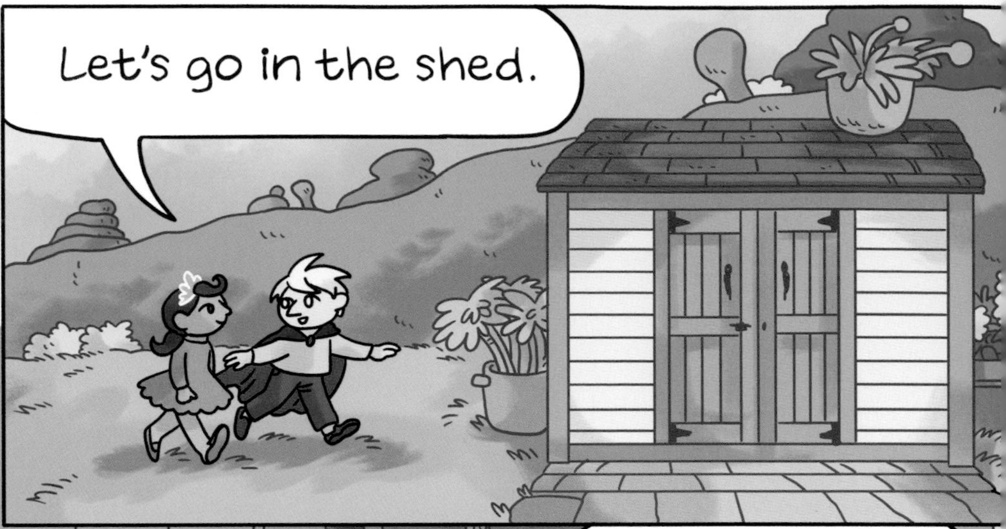
Let's go in the shed.

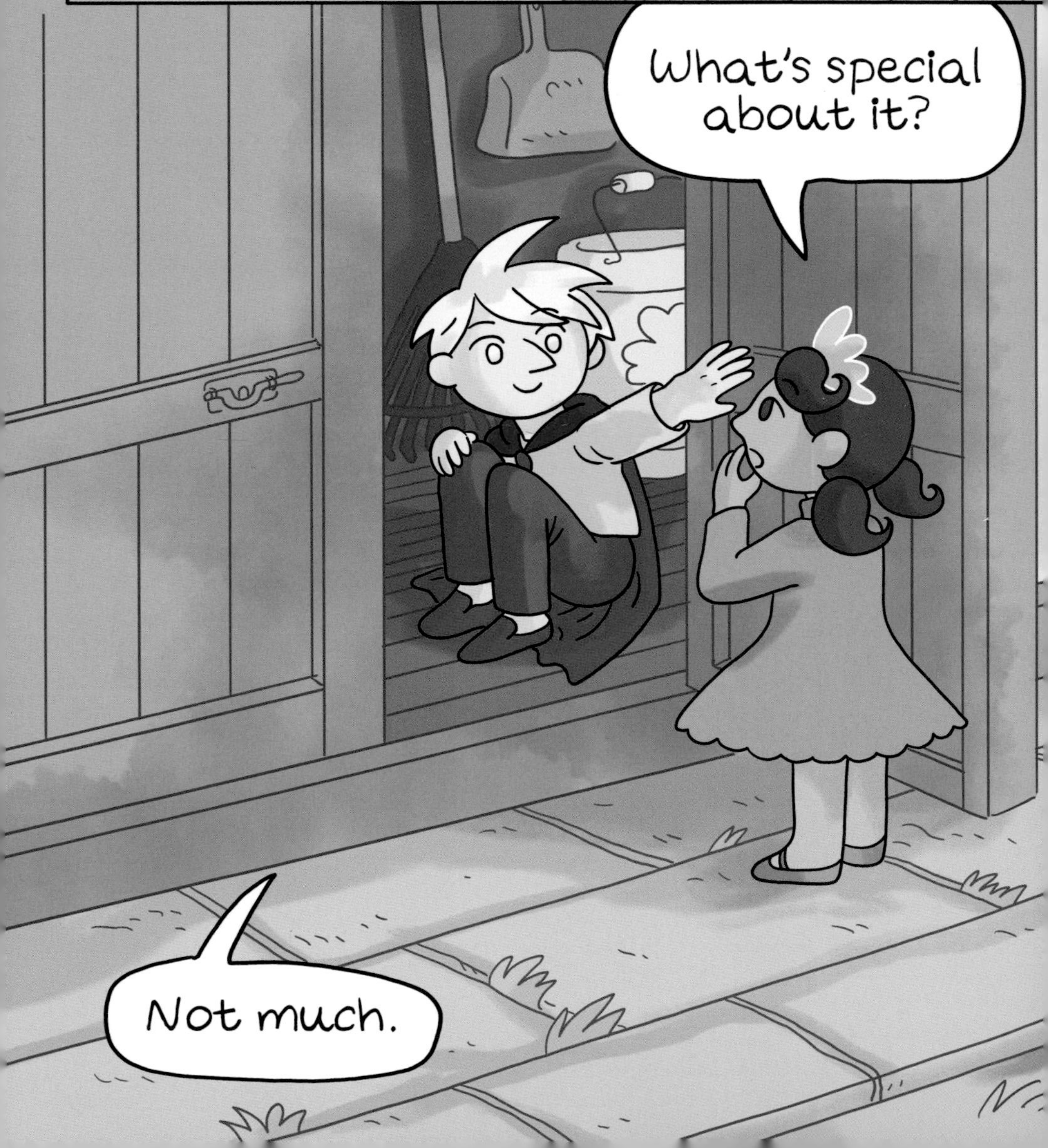
What's special about it?
Not much.

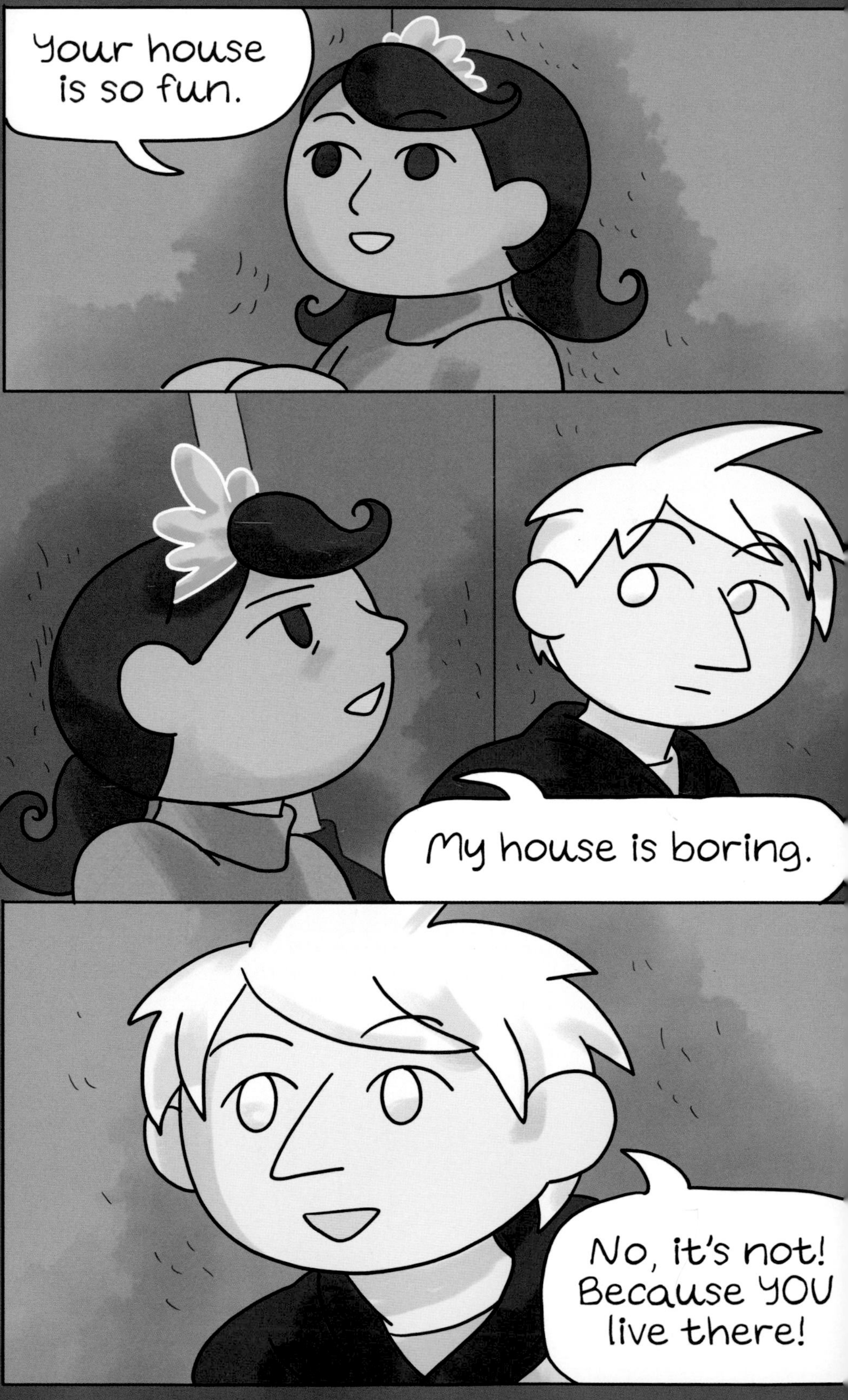
Your house is so fun.
My house is boring.
No, it's not! Because YOU live there!

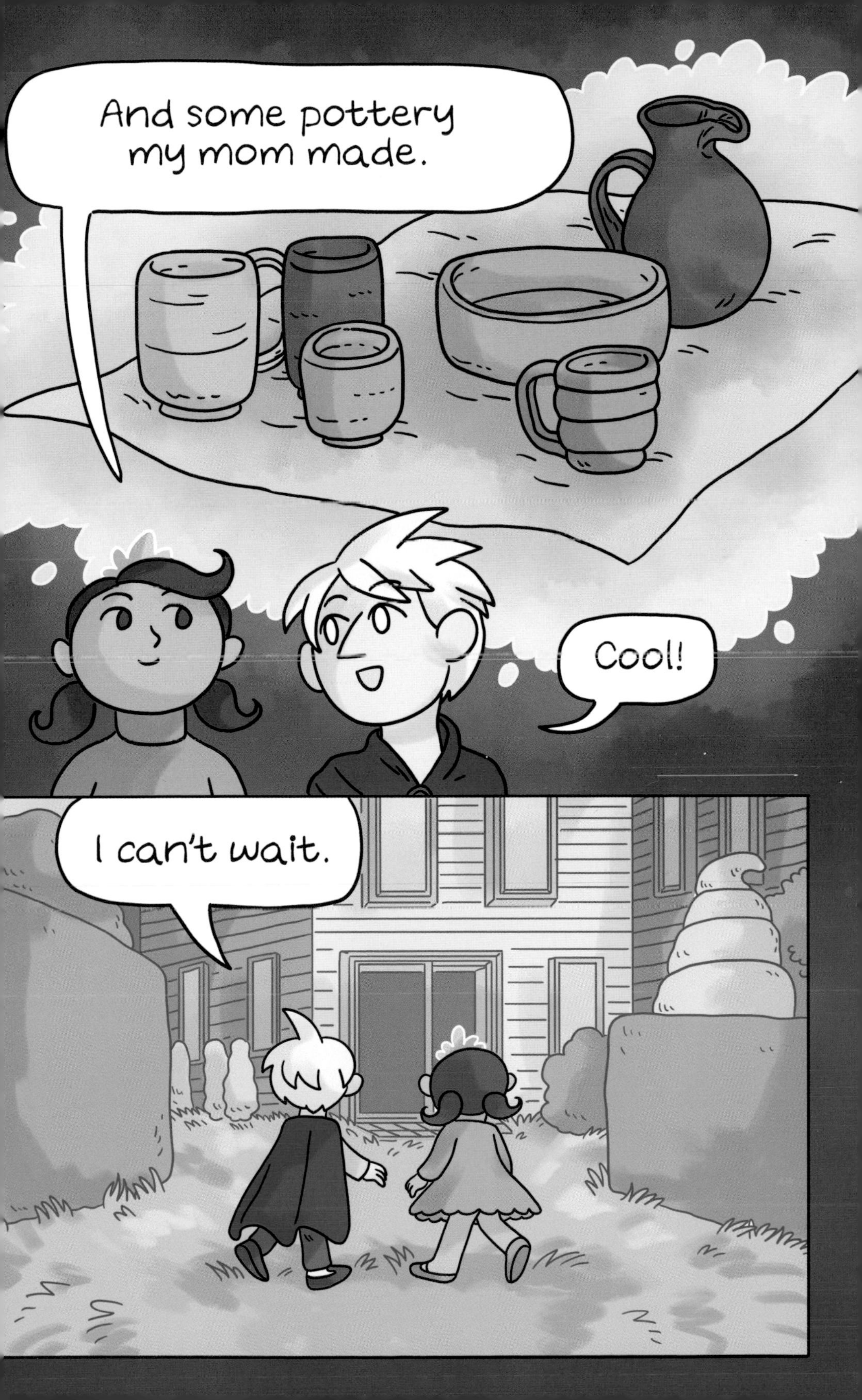
And some pottery my mom made.
Cool!
I can't wait.

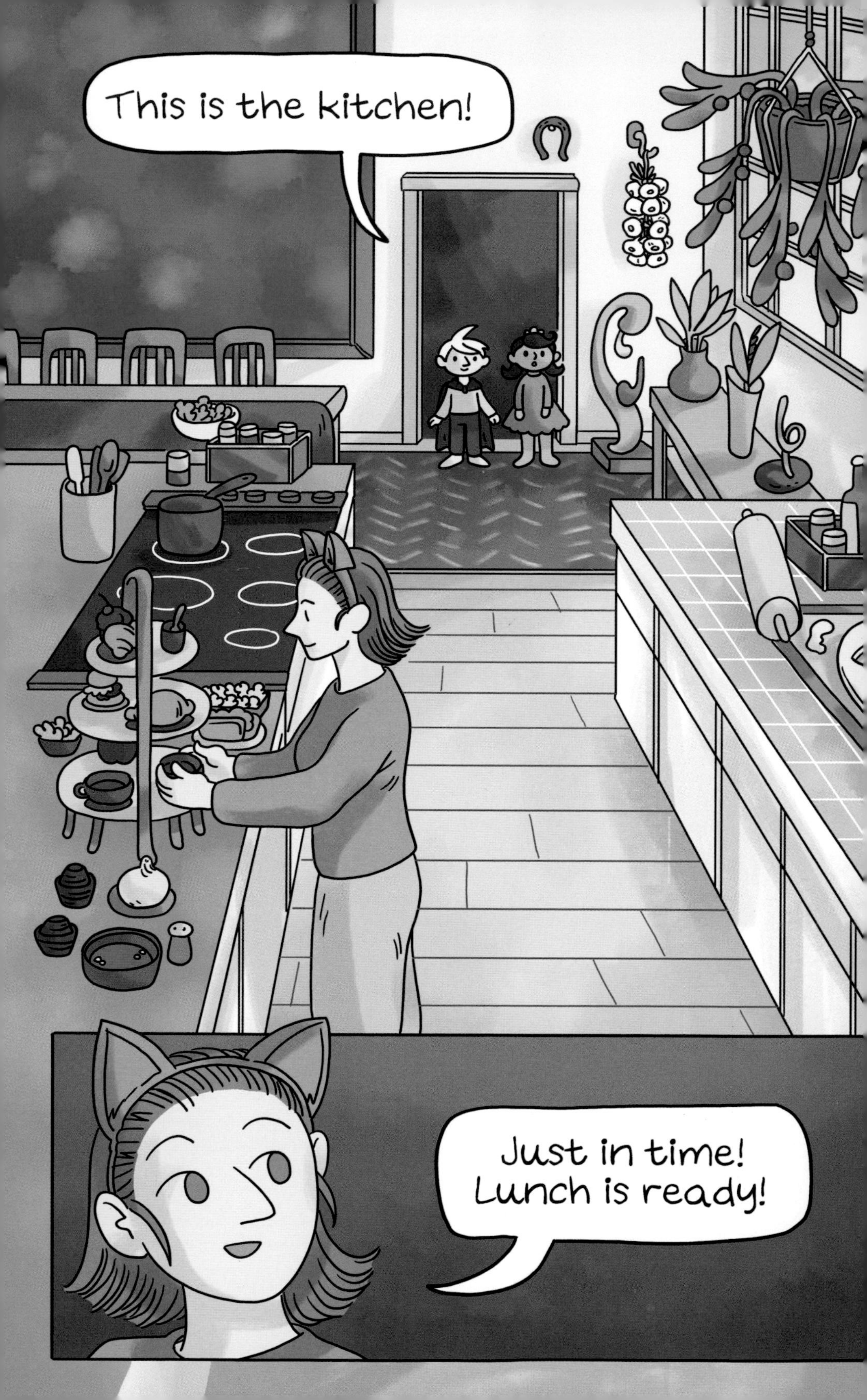
This is the kitchen!
Just in time!
Lunch is ready!

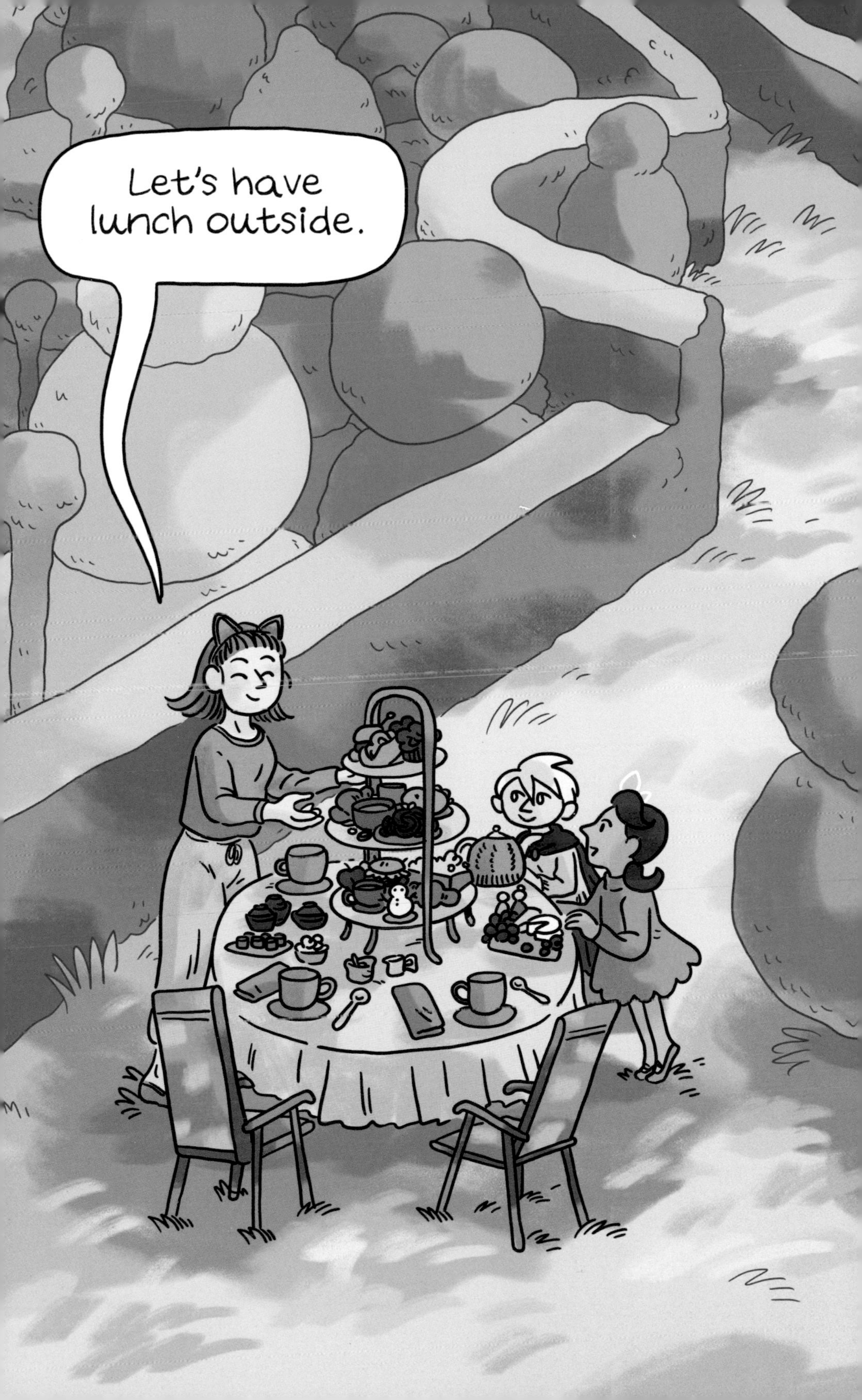
Let's have lunch outside.

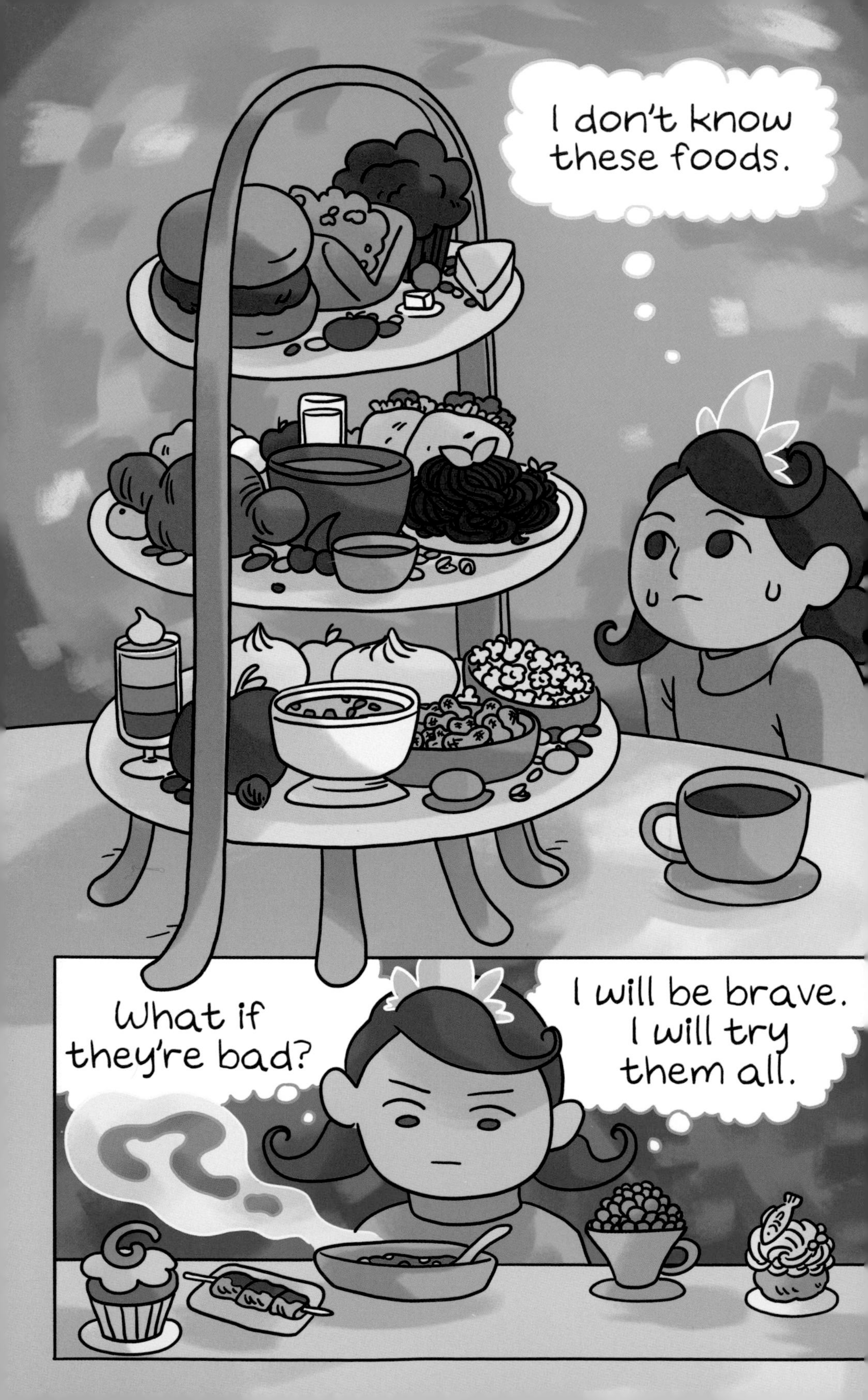

I don't know these foods.
What if they're bad?
I will be brave. I will try them all.

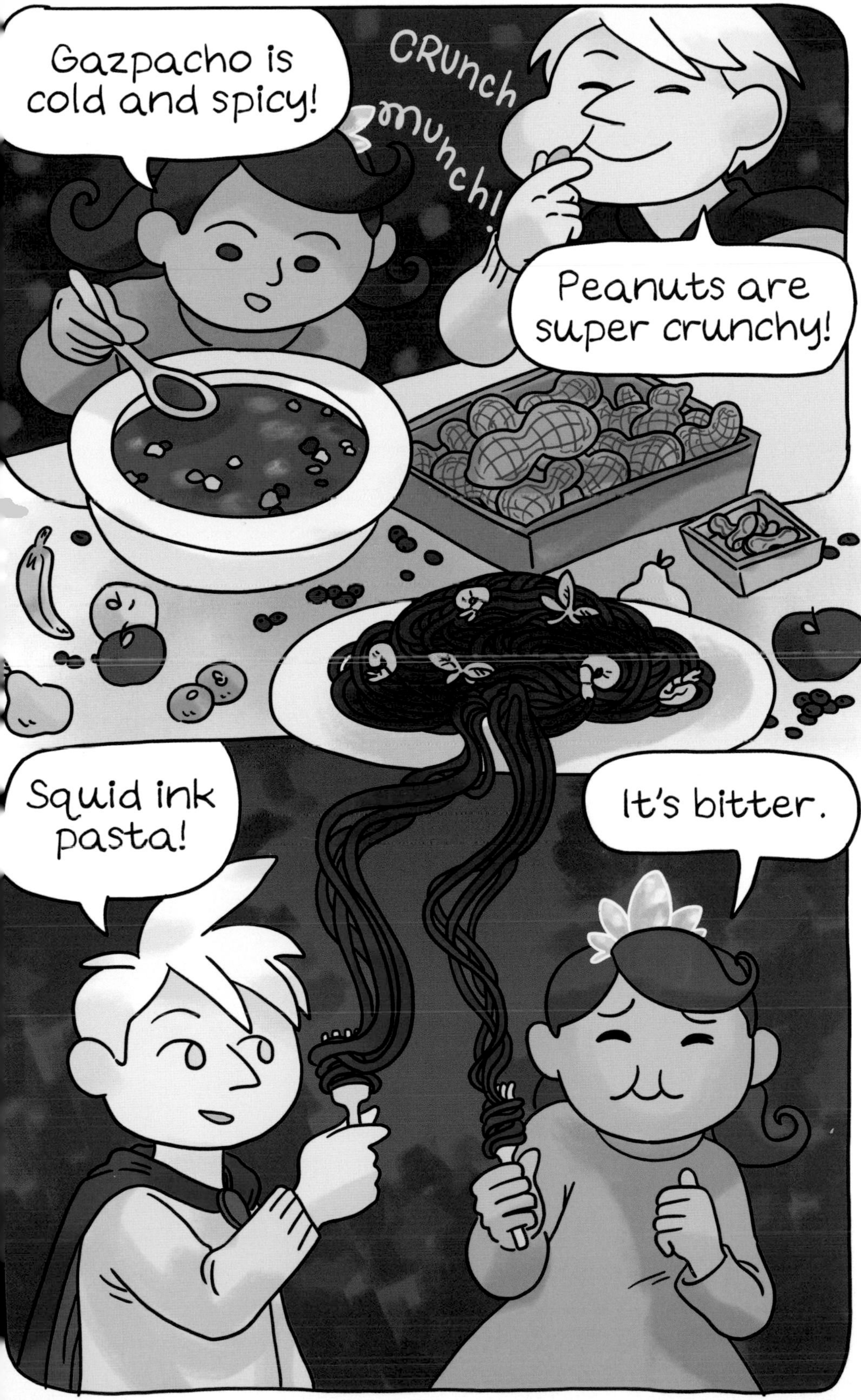
Gazpacho is cold and spicy!
CRUNCH
munch!
Peanuts are super crunchy!
Squid ink pasta!
It's bitter.

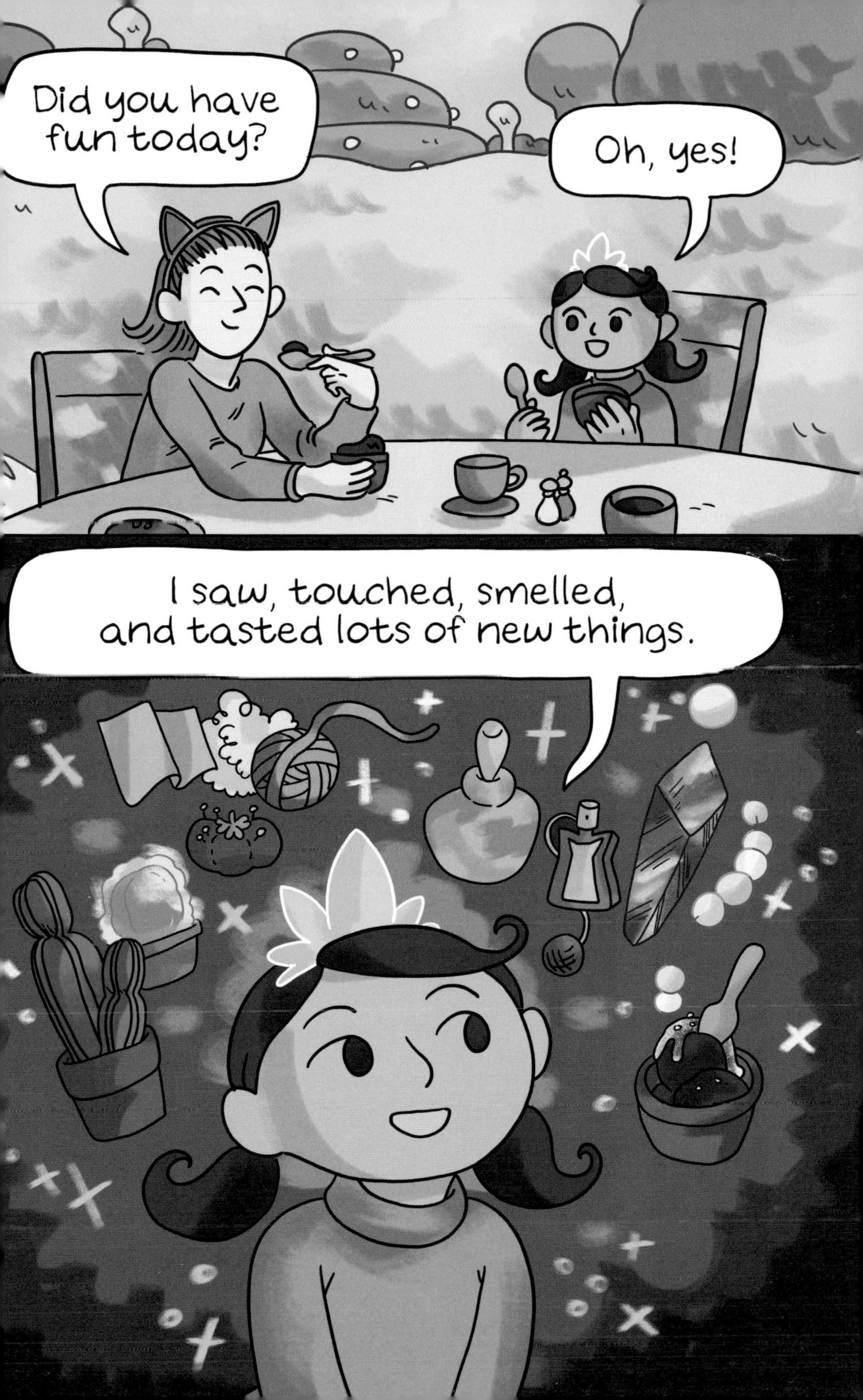
Did you have fun today?
Oh, yes!
I saw, touched, smelled, and tasted lots of new things.